Put Beginning Readers on the Right Track with
ALL ABOARD READING™

The All Aboard Reading series is especially designed for beginning readers. Written by noted authors and illustrated in full color, these are books that children really want to read—books to excite their imagination, expand their interests, make them laugh, and support their feelings. With fiction and nonfiction stories that are high interest and curriculum-related, All Aboard Reading books offer something for every young reader. And with four different reading levels, the All Aboard Reading series lets you choose which books are most appropriate for your children and their growing abilities.

Picture Readers
Picture Readers have super-simple texts, with many nouns appearing as rebus pictures. At the end of each book are 24 flash cards—on one side is a rebus picture; on the other side is the written-out word.

Station Stop 1
Station Stop 1 books are best for children who have just begun to read. Simple words and big type make these early reading experiences more comfortable. Picture clues help children to figure out the words on the page. Lots of repetition throughout the text helps children to predict the next word or phrase—an essential step in developing word recognition.

Station Stop 2
Station Stop 2 books are written specifically for children who are reading with help. Short sentences make it easier for early readers to understand what they are reading. Simple plots and simple dialogue help children with reading comprehension.

Station Stop 3
Station Stop 3 books are perfect for children who are reading alone. With longer text and harder words, these books appeal to children who have mastered basic reading skills. More complex stories captivate children who are ready for more challenging books.

In addition to All Aboard Reading books, look for All Aboard Math Readers™ (fiction stories that teach math concepts children are learning in school); All Aboard Science Readers™ (nonfiction books that explore the most fascinating science topics in age-appropriate language); and All Aboard Poetry Readers™ (funny, rhyming poems for readers of all levels).

All Aboard for happy reading!

D1057200

GROSSET & DUNLAP
Published by the Penguin Group
Penguin Group (USA) Inc., 375 Hudson Street, New York, New York 10014, U.S.A.
Penguin Group (Canada), 10 Alcorn Avenue, Toronto, Ontario, Canada M4V 3B2
(a division of Pearson Penguin Canada Inc.)
Penguin Books Ltd, 80 Strand, London WC2R 0RL, England
Penguin Ireland, 25 St Stephen's Green, Dublin 2, Ireland
(a division of Penguin Books Ltd)
Penguin Group (Australia), 250 Camberwell Road, Camberwell, Victoria 3124, Australia
(a division of Pearson Australia Group Pty Ltd)
Penguin Books India Pvt Ltd, 11 Community Centre, Panchsheel Park,
New Delhi - 110 017, India
Penguin Group (NZ), Cnr Airborne and Rosedale Roads, Albany,
Auckland 1310, New Zealand
(a division of Pearson New Zealand Ltd)
Penguin Books (South Africa) (Pty) Ltd, 24 Sturdee Avenue, Rosebank,
Johannesburg 2196, South Africa

Penguin Books Ltd, Registered Offices:
80 Strand, London WC2R 0RL, England

Dick and Jane® is a registered trademark of Addison-Wesley Educational Publishers, Inc. Copyright © 2005 by Pearson Education, Inc. All rights reserved. Published by Grosset & Dunlap, a division of Penguin Young Readers Group, 345 Hudson Street, New York, New York 10014. GROSSET & DUNLAP and ALL ABOARD READING are trademarks of Penguin Group (USA) Inc. Printed in the U.S.A.

ISBN 0-448-43980-8   10 9 8 7 6 5 4 3 2 1

ALL ABOARD READING™

with **24** Flash Cards!

PICTURE READER

Dick and Jane

Firehouse Field Trip

By Danielle M. Denega
Illustrated by Larry Ruppert

Grosset & Dunlap

"Time to go, !

Time to go, !

Time to board the .

Time to board the

for our field trip

to the ,"

said the .

Look! Look, !

Look at the  .

Look at the red  !

Oh! Oh, !

See the !

See the friendly !

Welcome!

Welcome to the .

This is our firehouse .

I am a !

I work at the .

Hear the  .

Hear the  ring.

When the  rings

there is a  !

There is a  at a  .

Look! Look at !

See slide down

the fire .

See slide down

the fire like a !

Oh,  .

Funny, funny  !

See wear a

firefighter's .

See the in his .

See him in his .

Look, Father!

Look at the .

The uses the .

The is used

to break a .

The is used

to break a .

See  !

See  in the .

See the .

See the truck's big !

Hear the horn!

Hear the sound its horn!

The have to move to the side.

The have to make way for the !

Firefighters spray a .

Firefighters spray

from a .

 puts the out!

Oh! Oh, !

I want to be a !

Oh! Oh, !

I want to be a !

 can be our dog!

Dick	Jane
teacher	bus
firehouse	fire truck

firefighter	dog
fire bell	pole
fire	helmet

boots	coat
house	ladder
hose	wheels

ax	water
cars	door
window	Spot